To Trick a God

H. Rad Bethlen

Rooster & Raven

roosterandravenpublishing.com
hradbethlen.com

For the Daughters of Zeus and Mnemosyne

Author Statement Concerning Artificial Intelligence

The way I write consist of several phases.

1. Idea generation.
2. Research.
3. Story development.
4. Outlining.
5. Writing the rough draft.
6. Editing and rewriting.
7. Editing and polishing.
8. Copy editing.

I will *occasionally* use AI during the research phase if I can't locate some bit of information on my own—but I try to locate it on my own first.

I will *occasionally* use AI during the story's development if I get stuck on something—but I try to resolve my own story issues first.

I *intentionally* use AI during the copy editing phase as a stand-in for a copy editor, which I can't afford to pay for yet which I don't want to go without.

A copy editor is the last set of eyes to look at a manuscript to check for grammar, usage, spelling, and punctuation mistakes. I ask the AI copy editor to make suggestions on corrections. I evaluate those suggestions. If I agree, I make the changes.

I don't use AI for anything else.

Be comforted that this story was written by a human being for other human beings.

H. Rad Bethlen

I have not heard your pleas in a long time, Maret.

"I need you."

Need?

"Devinti is dead. The young are clever, cruel, and desperate."

The children of the revolution turn on their parents?

"Yes."

You fear them?

"Yes."

Destroy them.

"They are endless."

Doubt? From you?

"One must consider failure."

Meaning?

"What will become of me after death? I have sinned."

How does one escape the repercussions of one's actions?

"I'm asking you."

. . .

He stood behind Maret. He never faced her. Not even preternatural speed, lent to her by magic, could move her fast enough to catch sight of him. He had always been and would always remain a mystery.

"Can he do it?" she asked.

I can think of no other.

"Will he?"

From behind—silence.

"The price?"

From behind—laughter.

"Take me to him."

. . .

The valley was a cornucopia of verdant life. There was barely room enough to pass—the flora pressed. The air was dense with fragrance. Countless birds fluttered from branch to branch, disappearing into pockets of sun-edged shadow. A copper-colored fox passed by Maret and her companion, brushing against them. He stopped to sniff Maret's bare ankle before ducking under a cluster of drooping dock leaves.

"Here?" asked Maret, incredulous.

A cave.

Maret folded back the leaves and branches. She slipped her bare toes beneath delicate flowers, her sandals tucked under her left arm. She was afraid to snap a twig, crush a blossom. She was afraid even of scuffing moss from a stone. Who knew what might anger him? With agonizing care she crossed the valley floor. As she approached the base of the cliff she saw the shadowed hollow. It was tall and narrow, like a black-bladed dagger thrust up from the earth, lodging itself in the stone. She paused.

Butterflies danced before her, flitting through the air. She watched them—annoyed. When they passed she intoned a spell. It was a simple cantrip, one that alerted her to the presence of magic auras. Her senses exploded. It was *all* magic. She clenched her eyes shut and ended the spell. After a minute of dazed and wobbling uncertainty her senses regained their courage and function. She heard chuckling behind her and ignored it.

She slipped sideways into the narrow cave. It curled into the stone. She was forced to shimmy herself along, smashing her breasts, scrapping her knees, wedging herself deeper and deeper until she could go no further. 'At least *he's* not behind me,' she mused. She glanced to her side. If the demon with whom she had long ago struck a bargain had followed, she would finally lay eyes on him. There was only darkness. She began a minor spell. The humid darkness of the cave was dispelled as the flickering light came into existence.

Maret would have leapt in surprise, were she not held immobile by the stone. She was face-to-face with another. As she calmed and took in more visual information she discerned that what she had taken to be another fully realized presence was nothing but a face carved in the stone, a partial face at that. A small section of the cave wall had been pressed back into a concave shape. Rising out of this bowl was the broad forehead, heavy eyebrows, high-arched nose, and square cheeks of an aristocratic face. It was as if a clay-worker had come into the cave, pressed her thumbs into the stone, and left her work incomplete.

The eyes opened and stared with stony indifference.

"I—" Began Maret.

Emotion overcame the face: profound sadness. The "skin" around the eyes crinkled. The muscles that directed the cheeks pulled them taunt. If stone could weep it would have. The emotion reversed, returning to normal. A moment later came irritation. The brow furrowed, the eyes narrowed. The anger was subdued but present. The effects of the emotions were so complete they nearly silenced Maret. She was, however, a woman not easily silenced.

"—need a shabti."

The face lifted, grinding, moving against itself, until a pair of broad, sculptural lips came into view.

"A vessel?" asked the face of stone. The trio of syllables came ponderously, echoing in the small space.

"Yes."

"To contain?" Again the trio reverberated.

"Sin," said Maret.

"Sin?" asked the face of stone.

"Can you make such a thing?"

The mouth curled downwards. The face sank, the lower half disappearing beneath the thumb-pressed stone. The eyes closed.

"I fear death," admitted Maret.

He made no response.

"I fear," she searched, "judgment."

The face emerged fully. The eyes opened.

"I've lived more than two centuries," began Maret. She appeared in her mid-twenties—part of the bargain. "I've made a pact with a demon. I've slaughtered hundreds, thwarted the fates of thousands, subjected entire peoples to tyranny." The face remained blank from emotion. "What awaits me?" Maret studied the face in the stone, the face *of* stone. It fluctuated between the lifeless chill of sculpture and the animated warmth of life. The features did not move. It was merely energy, consciousness, that seemed to come and go. Even when this consciousness came, was present, there came no response to Maret's plea. She made another.

"Will I be judged?"

Something affected the eyes. Again, not material, but energy. The word "judged" brought forth a heightened consciousness. Despite this, the stone did not speak.

"I want a shabti to take my place," said Maret, "to be judged, to be punished."

"You want to trick a god?" asked the face of stone.

"Can it be done?" asked Maret.

The face grew contemplative. Silenced reigned for some time. "She judges every soul that passes beneath her never-blinking gaze," said the face of stone. "Each soul is naked before her."

"It can't be done," said Maret, defeated. The full weight of her sin bore down upon her.

"A man beholds a river," said the face in the stone, his deep voice resonating in the small space. "He cups his hand, he drinks. The river is in this man, wherever he goes." The face did not elaborate.

Maret, baffled by the metaphor, asked, "Meaning?"

"What *is* a soul?" asked the stone face.

"I don't—"

"If a soul be a river, can the soul be drawn from? If drawn from, what becomes of that which is taken away?"

Maret could not answer.

"There is but one soul, one river—divided—to which all drops return. First," the face fell silent, studying Maret with hard eyes, "these drops must be—purified—before they return home. *This* is what you fear."

"Yes," admitted Maret.

"It follows," continued the face of stone, "that to be purified in advance is what you wish."

"The shabti?"

"To gather the water which you have fouled, to separate it from the clean. To subject it to—purification." The stone eyes regarded Maret. "This *can* be done."

"Yes!" Maret was giddy. The silence of the stone face dampened her premature celebration. She studied it. "The price?" She could only whisper the question.

"All water returns to the river," said the sculpted face. "Yet not all water takes the same path home."

Maret grew nervous.

"I *can* draw the brackish from the fresh. For this, I will have a handful to raise to *my* lips."

...

What does it mean to be created?

The voice echoed in her mind, although she had no concept of self.

We must be told of being born for we remember nothing.

The voice, deep, resonating, stoic, yet tinted with disappointment and melancholy, was the only thing she knew. It was all that existed. As each word appeared it was defined, comprehended.

Perhaps it is better, for memory is a fickle friend.

A pause. In the silence there was only darkness, nothingness, an imperfect vacuum. Into this void she, having no name, no self, projected only curiosity. The voice had awakened her. In its absence she searched for what else might be.

You will know of your own creation, your own arrival into the physical plane. Know you that these words are not your own? How could you? First, I must situate you in *something, so you know where you stop.*

She was aware of physicality. She could not picture it, only feel it. Its contours were entirely foreign. Its containment was alien and worrisome. She heard bizarre sounds, the mechanics of her organic systems. They meant nothing to her. She could not place them. They simply existed and she knew they were a part of her. This awareness was followed by still more. She became aware of drawing breath. She became aware of a pump working at the core of her being. She immediately grew fond of the regularity of its action, the singularity of its purpose.

She became aware of the sense of touch. She was aware of something hard and cold beneath her. She was aware from this that she herself was not hard and cold, but its opposite. She felt that there were a grouping of spots, at either side of her, at the ends of twin extensions, more sensitive than the rest. She sought out new sensations. She moved.

She became aware, without definitions, causes, reasons, that she was a collection of natural laws, prescribed actions and reactions, that she, via some unknown power, could command. Even if this command was limited and mysterious, fraught with hazard, it was hers. This awareness filled her with a quiet, beaming happiness, a mystical, spiritual contentment. She had a home.

You begin to understand.

Yes.

She was shocked by her own response. It was inside her. It *was* her. A voice separate from the voice that had authored her with the power of its word. She felt there was more possible. "Yes," she said aloud. The action thrilled her. She learned of her ears. As she spoke, as she breathed in and out, she tasted the air. It was moist, earthen, metallic. She became aware of its odor, musky, organic, and with it her own smell, the smell of her flesh, her hair.

There is one last sense. The one your kind rely on the most.

A soft glow began at the corner of her eyes. The fragments of light reached out and up, forming a halo that grew into a dome. Her eyes worked to make sense of this new information. The fuzzy, indistinct dome of light began to sharpen, gradate, form planes, curves, solid shapes. She knew, the knowledge came to her, that she was in a cave. The planes formed rocks. She was lying on a long, flat rock. The characteristics of the rock she already knew. She knew then that other material things would have their own characteristics, just as she had hers.

She became aware of him. She turned her head and studied him. He too seemed to be made of rock. She wondered if her own shape was like his, elongated, tapering, solid in the middle with protrusions, extensions. She turned and looked down at her own body. It was similar to his but different in a multitude of ways.

"I can read your thoughts."

The voice was no longer in her head but outside of it. She looked again at the stone man.

"Fascinating."

She had watched his lips move. "Fascinating," she repeated, moving her lips. She smiled at the odd feeling of speech, it moved her face, constricted her throat. It was bizarre. When she fell silent the sensations stopped.

She was aware that he was sad. She did not know how she knew this. It had to be something in the way he stood, the way his head bent, the way his features changed. "Already, your mind begins to close. You are becoming limited by your physical existence."

"Limited?" She could not place his complicated, intertwined emotions. "Why?"

He turned away, paced the cave, ignoring her question. He stopped, gazed at her. "I am your creator." She wanted to ask why to this as well, why he had created her, but felt he would give her that same enigmatic look. "You are perfect." He spun to face her. "I am pleased to have made you, pleased to have experienced your first moments." He paused, looking at her. "I am pleased that you exist. You shall fulfill your purpose, your destiny." He stepped forward, stopping beside her. "So few do." He grew sullen. He studied her nude form, his handiwork. His mood lifted. "You shall be like the earth. You shall accept the seed and bring it to fruition."

She laid her head back on the stone and looked up at the concave ceiling. His speech made little sense to her. Two words struck her as poignant, however. "Purpose?" She tilted her head and looked into his face. "Destiny?"

He lifted his stony arm, extended a rough-hewn finger. "To suffer." He touched his finger to her forehead.

. . .

She heard frantic screams. Her eyes were closed. Her nostrils filled with alien, alarming odors; the stench of sweat, of fear, and something she couldn't place; metallic, organic. She held opposites. Whatever was in her left hand was soft yet firm, warm but rapidly cooling, and slippery.

Whatever was in her right hand was cold, hard, unforgiving, dangerous. She opened her eyes. She knew one object to be a knife. Like with everything said in the cave, the meaning came to her. She looked to her other hand—a human heart. She glanced down at her feet—a corpse.

In looking down she saw herself as well. White cloth, now stained red, draped around her, held from gold chains that rest on her slender shoulders. She looked out over the crowd. She was standing on a stone platform, the crowd prostrate beneath her. She held aloft the heart, blood running down her arm, warm and slick. She squeezed, spurting blood from the arteries which splashed on her shoulders, breasts, face. It tasted like iron. The crowd looked up, yelled, and prostrate themselves again. The stone and the crowd was in a clearing surrounded by simple huts and behind them dense jungle.

Another. Whispered the voice in her ear. *Tell them, Cyth-V'sug will corrupt the soil, poison the air. Tell them, Angazhan will turn the jungle against them. Tell them, Barbatus will anger the beasts. These foul acts will happen unless the blood flows. Unless their souls are given.*

Maret told them. She sacrificed another.

. . .

She was once again in darkness. The cool, solid bulk of the stone was beneath her. She was disoriented. She blinked and tried to see but couldn't. Other than the feel of the stone there was nothing. She became aware of his presence.

"Can you make light?" she asked.

"I do not wish to."

Although his voice reverberated from the stone walls she was able to place him. He was sitting on the floor, his back against the stone she lie upon. She reached out, felt for him. She found the curve of his shoulder by twisting her arm. Feeling pain, she straightened it.

"I am Maret," she stated.

He did not respond.

"I control a people," she continued. "From them, I make many offerings." She paused, attempting to understand what that meant. "To please demons. I care not if my people suffer or die. I don't care about," she paused again, searching, "anyone but myself."

"Not you."

"Who?" she asked, not understanding.

She heard movement. She knew he had stood. She felt the cool, hard touch of his finger on her forehead.

. . .

You cannot miss them, Maret.

She stood on the balcony, looking out over An, the "City of Triangles"; the skyline dominated by pyramidal tombs, now shinning deep red in the setting sun. The buildings of An were made of sandstone, the streets paved with the same. Colorful awnings broke the brown-bronze monotony. Long ago, An had been a city of slaves, an unwilling army to build the tombs. Now it was a city of laborers, merchants, free men and women, foreigners, travelers, adventurers. Lights began to flare in the shadows of the city streets as the bronze-colored sun broke the horizon, dragging a blanket of star-punctured indigo behind it.

"Get out of my head."

Tell me, what is it you miss about those savages?

"I miss them. That's all," said Maret. "They were like children, innocent and trusting."

They were currency, to be spent.

"They trusted me to lead them, to keep them safe."

They are safe.

As he said this, the gem, placed on a golden chain hung around her neck, pulsed with light and warmth. Contained within were hundreds of souls, a small portion of the souls of those she had sacrificed. The majority of her offerings went to others, to foul demon lords thrashing in the Abyss. The one who advised her, with whom she had struck a bargain from which there was no escape, took his share. What remained after the gluttonous consuming, like crumbs from a cake, were hers. She heard their muted cries of anguish, anguishing for freedom. She had worn many such gems on her person. Unfortunately, she had been forced to part with all but one. That she was still alive and still possessed even a single such gem was due to *him*.

While walking in the Footprints of Rovagug, in the desert south of the Scarab River, passing from West to East Osirion, she had confronted a terrible sight.

She took it for an abandoned holy marker, some sign of a long forgotten ancient civilization, nearly buried under the wind-shaped dunes. It curved into the cloudless sky, a pillar of gold, with a barb at the top the length of a man. What lie buried at its base she did not know, but was soon to find out.

As she approached to examine the pillar of gold the sand shook beneath her, throwing her from her feet. She scooted away as the pillar curled, aiming its barb at her. What emerged from the sand was as frightening as it was dangerous. It was a golden-colored scorpion that towered over her, dropping her into shadow. What she had taken for a pillar was its tail. Its pincers were crystalline, the color of rubies, with edges as sharp as cut glass. On its back were hundreds, if not thousands, of baby scorpions, each the span of her hand. They writhed, climbing over one another, a living blanket. As if these sights were not terrifying enough the golden scorpion's head was not that of its kind, but a twisted, discolored, fearsome human head, a woman's head, devoid of any hair, but with long fangs and a serpent's air-tasting tongue.

"Aldinach!" he screamed.

Whether *he* was screaming the scorpion's name to her, or addressing the demon lord of sand, scorpions, and thirst herself, Maret was not sure. Maret rose, backing cautiously away. Aldinach looked just over Maret's shoulder, where *he* was undoubtedly revealing his presence, seemed to frown, then looked back at Maret. She advanced, lowering a massive pincer.

"You've ventured far from the Whispering Sands," he said. "Careful your sister doesn't reclaim them in your absence."

Aldinach paused. She once more gazed just beyond Maret's shoulder. She seemed to be assessing *him*. She turned back to Maret. "You have souls," she said, her voice like quicksand swallowing a panicking victim.

"They aren't for you," said Maret, before she could think not to.

Her defensive outcry amused the lord of scorpions. She advanced another step, her tail curling, a drop of poison clinging to the tip of her barb. "How shall you keep them from me?"

"Do you mean to pose a riddle?" He said. "Is that not your sister's vocation?"

"Speak once more of her," hissed Aldinach, staring just past Maret. "And I shall—"

"Can you be certain?" he asked, interrupting the demon lord. "What of my alliance?"

"You are nothing, a pathetic time-server, a—"

"Perhaps, but it is *whom* I serve, not that I serve."

Aldinach paused, tasting the air with her split tongue, her pincers restlessly clacking, the living blanket of scorpions on her back convulsing in anger. She seemed to smile. "He hasn't appeared to save you. Will he?"

"Undoubtedly not," he said.

"What have I to fear from you, or your," her lips curled into a sneer, "alliance?"

"Actions have repercussions."

"Is there not enough hot air in the desert?" asked Aldinach. "Must you contribute—"

"You can take your chances," he said, undaunted. "Or, perhaps, a compromise?"

"I have not come to compromise, but to take."

"Take you could," he said. "You are the great and feared Aldinach, who drove her sister from her home, whose cult is as vast and as plentiful as all the sand in all the deserts of the multiverse. Still," he seemed to sneer a caveat, "you would risk much for little."

"Souls are no paltry prize," said Aldinach.

"True, and we have gathered many. Take some, a gift from us to you, for the privilege of walking upon your sands. Yet, leave us some, and leave us our lives, so that we may praise you."

Aldinach laughed. "You speak with his honeyed tongue. He has taught you to grovel well."

"Grovel?" he asked. "No, he would not permit me. I praise and offer a gift. Take these souls and use them as you will. Leave us half and our lives. It is a generous gift."

"To me? Or to you?" She laughed again. "I can take." She looked at Maret, who was crouching in the shadow of one of Aldinach's massive pincers, a spell at the ready, a spell, she surmised, that, for all its potency, would do nothing to so powerful an entity as Aldinach.

He made no response.

Aldinach looked back and forth between Maret and the one behind her.

"A clerk," she sneered. "A taker of notes, a keeper of catalogs." She brought her barb closer. The poison threatened to fall. "The tyranny of the bureaucrat. The boredom of a librarian bereft of books." This seemed to amuse her. "Still, *he* is great, even if *you* are weak. I accept your gift. Not half. Ha! You may keep." Her pincer shot out, the tip speeding toward Maret's heart. At the last moment it angled up and knocked against the largest of her gems, the one at her throat. Aldinach smiled. The scorpions on her back danced with triumphant jubilation. "The rest," her pincer moved down Maret's body, stopping at her wrist. With surprising dexterity for such a bulky "digit," she plucked the bracelets from both Maret's wrists. The gems, containing a hundred souls each, sparkled as the desert sun shone through them. "Are mine."

"It is a pleasure to give," he said.

. . .

"It was a defeat," said Maret.

You fail to appreciate how lucky we are to be alive.

"I thought you were powerful."

I am.

"Ha! That wasn't power, it was guile, artfulness. We lost a century worth of—"

It was a set back, yes, but we shall persevere.

"Will the guardian even accept what we have? What remains is so little."

A soul is a soul.

"You didn't answer my question."

We can offer and ask. Our options were always thus.

"Except we have a fraction of what we had before. Our offering might insult her."

Then you die.

"Thanks."

. . .

Maret stood within the largest of An's pyramidal tombs. The corpse of the tomb robber, that had revealed to her the secret tunnel that led within, was lying in the corner, his decapitated head in his lap, the gold Maret had given him still in his purse. Maret stared up at the massive beams of stone overhead. She lifted her hand. The six orbs of magical light that she had summoned floated closer to the beams. "Impossible."

How many slaves do you think it took—

"Slaves?" She shook her head. "No amount of slaves could lift those stones."

Some mechanism lost to time? Some techniques man has become ignorant of?

"Perhaps. But what?"

It could be that the Pharaoh's magic was potent enough —

Maret laughed. "Only if he truly was a god." She directed the lights away from the beams to the walls. "If he were a god—he wouldn't need a tomb." She stepped to the wall and studied the hieroglyphs. After several hours of deciphering the riddle contained within the symbols, she stepped to the middle of the room and began the incantation, speaking in the forbidden tongue, forbidden, that is, to mortals, thus to her. When she was done she looked around her. Nothing happened.

"Did I misspeak?"

Not that I could tell.

"Then—"

Perhaps, try again—

The entire pyramid shook. Dust fell from the massive stone beams above. A portion of the wall slid back and down. The shaking ceased.

Or, perhaps, patience.

Maret looked to the darkened doorway. She directed the lights to it and saw a set of stairs leading up. She went. The stairs turned and continued to an opening a third the height of a normal door. She was obliged to crawl through. She stood on the other side and at once saw the room's occupant.

She appeared to be sitting at a table, the flame from a brass oil lamp illuminating a book as well as her angular face. She wore a loose fitting top of pure white cotton. Around her neck was a thick gold necklace studded with gems. Her straight, black hair, four feet in length, glistened in the light. She looked up at Maret, her eyes reflecting the flame's flickering light. She looked over Maret's shoulder, seeing what Maret could not. She was nonplused at the sight of unexpected visitors. She moved her hand over the open pages. Her nails, being several inches long and arriving at points, threatened to slice through the ancient parchment. Maret at once dropped to her knees and lowered her forehead to the floor.

"Oh, great—"

A deafening roar filled the room. This was followed by the swishing of a tail. This sound of swishing came closer. Maret dare not lift her forehead from the floor. Out of the corners of her eyes she saw the woman's lower half, that of a massive lion. The woman growled and Maret's magical orbs dissipated. Only the flickering glow of the oil lamp remained. The thick, black claws of the lamia's paws drug against Maret's skin, not enough to wound, but enough to warn. A human finger touched Maret's shoulder. Then the lamia turned and padded silently across the room. Maret rose, dusting off her knees. The lamia, her back turned to Maret, continued around the table. She bent, reached out, and pinched the wick between her fingers. The room fell dark. The lamia began to speak, her voice husky.

"Oh, Rovagug, may the sound of your voice shatter our worthless souls. Oh, Rovagug, may the pestilence of your breath waste away the flesh we so desperately cling to. Oh, Rovagug, reach up from the earth, open it, let us tumble into your hungry maw. Oh, Rovagug, spew fire from the mountain tops to rain upon our heads. Oh, Rovagug, he who devours, he who destroys. We beseech you. Destroy us! Destroy us! We are unworthy!"

Light poked through the darkness, the sight of distant fires. Maret could begin to make out a blasted landscape. She was no longer in the pyramidal tomb, no longer in An, or even on the material plane. She was in the Abyss. That hostile expanse had wormed its way as close to Rovagug's prison as was able, maybe in an attempt to free him, maybe out of sheer curiosity, or maybe for its own reasons, as the Abyss at times seemed malevolently alive.

Maret stood on a precipice, overlooking a vast range of volcanos, each of which spewed fire, smoke, and molten rock. From these angry peaks, lava flowed. The sky above was smoke-clouded. Red-yellow sparks fell like rain. The air was heavy with foul gasses and suffocating heat. Maret began a spell, completing it before she suffocated to death. With the spell, she could breathe, although with some pain.

The Abyssal lamia, part woman, part lion, part demon, looked out over the burning expanse, her face aglow. Maret stepped next to her and looked down. A sheer rock face dropped thousands of feet into a fast-flowing river of lava. She glanced at the lamia. The other woman had a look of longing in her smoky eyes.

"To join him," she whispered.

Maret backed away from the edge.

The Abyssal lamia turned. A spectacular eruption framed her. The boom of the exploding mountain top reverberated through the landscape, shaking the ground beneath Maret's feet. The lamia glanced over her shoulder, then turned back to Maret. "He acknowledges us." She looked to the sky, as if awaiting the arrival of some molten hunk of stone meant to obliterate them. When nothing came she turned back to Maret and held out her hand. Maret stepped forward, lifted the necklace, and placed it in the lamia's hand.

"Please accept this, Vaskilli." She lowered her eyes and backed away.

Vaskilli made no movement. She held out her hand as if she held something unworthy of her attention.

'The offering was not enough,' Maret silently cursed. 'It's all over.'

She figured herself for dead. She wondered what would happen to *him*. *He* was not a chosen of Rovagug and no mater what alliance *he* claimed, be it true or false, the god of endings would care not. She began to rapidly cycle through the spells she had memorized and the magical items she had on her person, looking for something to aid her, her drive for survival being that strong. '*He* won't risk helping me now.' She thought. Before she had fallen too far into panic, Vaskilli turned, her arm still extended. She stepped to the edge, turned over her wrist, and dropped the necklace and its soul gem over the edge of the precipice.

Maret could feel her heart pounding in her chest. The necklace took a painfully long time to fall. That it sunk in the lava, she had no doubt. A bluish glow came up from the edge of the cliff. Maret was astonished to see the souls that had once been contained within the gem float into view. The number was alarming. They vaguely resembled their bodily appearances. They collected at the edge of the precipice, floating out over the river of lava far below, and turned their eyes on Maret. They seemed ready to attack her, to revenge their betrayal, when Vaskilli pointed to a massive volcano.

The souls fought against her command, the anger they had toward Maret was powerful enough to hold them near. They inched forward, opening their mouths to accuse, lifting their hands to make their vengeance felt. Maret began a spell but halted when Vaskilli screamed in anger. The souls sped away, disappearing into the obscured sky above. The Abyssal lamia remained motionless, staring out over the expanse of volcanos. Maret, too, waited, for what she wasn't certain.

Vaskilli tilted her head, listening to a voice only she could hear. She remained this way for some time then turned to face Maret. Her tail began to tremble with excitement. She licked her lips, then smiled, revealing a mouth full of blood stained fangs. She began to crouch, an evil gleam coming to her dark eyes. Maret began a spell. Behind her she felt movement. Perhaps, she thought *he* wasn't as quick to abandon her as she had worried. The Abyssal lamia leapt forward, reaching out with both clawed hands.

. . .

She woke up screaming. The sound rebounded from the cave walls. She sat up, breathing hard, her skin clammy with sweat. She was sunk in darkness, unable even to see her hand before her eyes. As her panic faded she realized that she was no longer on the precipice, that the lamia was not charging toward her. Her breathing calmed and having nothing else to do she lay back down.

"What does it mean?" she asked. "Was I there? How did I come to be here, when I was there?" The sound of her own voice was still alien to her, a bit alarming, besides, it was not the voice she wished to hear. She turned onto her side and felt along the edge of the rock. He wasn't there.

. . .

He stood in the shadowed cavity of a banyan tree, hugged, like a stone captured by the tree's growth and lifted from the soil. He peered down into the valley, his eyes able to see through the flora is if it were transparent. He stared at the cave entrance. Her scream spilled out of the cave, an ill wind that portend storms. The birds nearby took flight. Beneath him, rabbits, who had been scratching their ears with their paws, shot off into the shadows. He closed his eyes and wept.

. . .

Velles awoke in his cell. He was disoriented. He was in semi-darkness. He was cold. The air stunk of old sweat, urine, and rats. His throat was sore. His body ached. He could barely remember where he was. The effect of weeks of unremitting fasting had been to disgorge him from space and time. He tried to remember why he had chosen self-banishment, why he now occupied a monk's lonely cell. *Atone*. 'Yes," he thought. 'I am atoning—" For what, he could not recall. He remembered standing before the Abbot.

The Abbot looked up from a scroll he was studying, but did not speak. He combed his white beard with a wrinkled hand. The age spots on his bald dome swallowed the candlelight. His eyes shone with the inner light of self-discipline. Distant chanting could be heard. In the streets below, the commerce of the day was conducted in hushed tones, so as not to disturb the holy men inside the ancient, repurposed citadel.

"My thoughts are unclean," said Velles. "I must—"

The Abbot ceased to comb his beard.

Velles stood up from the wooden plank. His ragged robe, stiff with grime, full of body lice, was rough against his flesh. He took a single step and arrived at the desk. The book was open to the final page. He had labored over the illustration for days, weeks perhaps, in a state of spiritual bliss. He turned and looked to the window at the top of the wall. He could not see out, but light came in, falling on the book. He had no real memory of making the illustration

He wasn't sure where he had acquired the colored inks, the greens and blues and vibrant yellows. He passed his hand over the assorted brushes. They had been used to excess, the bristles worn to nothing.

Authoring the book, writing every word with care, illustrating every page, had been his own idea, his means of atonement. He had meant to write the sacred words, to tell the sacred stories, to put the timeless parables into the mouths of the saints. While this was his intent, it was not the result. He had failed to duplicate the holy book of his god. He *had* succeeded in authoring a book like no other. There were none like it in his monastery's library—in any library—as far as he knew. At first, its contents were a mystery. He had written the words, like he had illustrated the final page, in a state that couldn't quite be called consciousness. It was not unconsciousness either, but something like being outside of his body. He had not been present, or so he thought, when the words had been written.

Where had he been?

Absent.

Then he read the book and understood.

He looked again at the window. He was a monk, a penitent, one who suffers for faith, not a priest or a cleric, one who spreads the faith. He did not have the gift of divine magic, had not sought it. He felt fear. Not fear of the magic itself, no, fear he could not be trusted with it. He knew his own thoughts. He knew the depth of the darkness within his soul. He had tried everything to rid himself of his burden; beating himself on his back and thighs with a scourge until his flesh flew in bloody strips; starving himself until his bones showed, praying and fasting for days on end. He had spent forty days in the desert east of Ecanus without food or water. He'd survived on sand beetles and faith. How he had survived he did not know. Still, the thoughts came.

Nothing helped. All his life he heard readers reading aloud to themselves from forbidden books. He heard records of travels to lands that could not exist and of what was seen in them. He caught pieces of eldritch magical formulae that he dare not comprehend. He heard truths buried beneath lies, obscured by half-truths. He heard descriptions of a false paradise in which true believers frolicked and by this he knew what they did not. He fled from these voices as one would run from a fiend, yet had never truly rid himself of them.

Then he read the book and understood.

He had written it for none other than himself.

It was his awakening.

A bite from a louse stirred him from his reverie. He felt disgust. He had been in the cell for how long? He had not bathed. He had lost a tremendous amount of weight. A second bite stirred him to action. He shed the robe and with his hands flung the lice from his skin. He stood naked in the shaft of light, looking over his own worn, filthy body.

"I've been a fool." For a moment he was angry at himself but soon realized there could have been no other way. He looked down at the illustration. "Abraxas," he whispered. He reached out and ran his fingertips over the portrait.

Abraxas was the demon lord of forbidden lore, magic, and snakes. What little of him that resembled human was the torso and arms. Even these were covered in a serpent's glistening scales. From the waste down his body formed a trunk which split into two massive serpents, their heads moving and acting as one with him. Abraxas's head was an unnatural hybrid of serpent and predatory bird. A brilliantly colored crest distracted viewers from the un-bird-like fangs and the eyeless sockets. Only yellow energy spilled from those twin holes.

A hiss caught Velles's attention. He turned and looked at his discarded robe. From between the filthy folds emerged a slick serpentine body. The scales of its head were coppery, twin black stripes ran lengthwise from just behind the eyes down the serpent's back. Velles turned and knelt. The serpent continued to emerge. Its length astonished Velles, as did its girth, for it was as thick as a man's arm.

The serpent slithered around his legs, between his legs, and spread itself until it occupied the totality of the cell's floor. Only then did it take any notice of him. It turned its head toward his hand. Velles extended his fingers. The serpent tasted the air. It then lifted its head to look up. Its eyes were dark, so dark that Velles could not see the slit pupils. So hard did the monk stare, so lost did he become in the serpent's luminous eyes, that he was not prepared for the bite. The serpent withdrew its fangs and lowered its head. Velles half-fell against the plank bed. He sunk to the floor. His last conscious thought was of the book.

. . .

The Abbot smelled something unpleasant. He was standing in the intersection of a hallway he rarely walked. He turned and looked to his left. The U-shaped hall was home to fifteen monk cells. He sniffed, frowned, then began down the hall. 'Perhaps someone is ill,' he thought. He rounded the first curve and saw an open door. That was not unusual, as none of the doors locked. The monks could come and go as they pleased, most chose not to. He stepped into the doorway and looked around the room. The smell was awful. The sun was low in the sky and there was little light to aid him.

The Abbot began a simple incantation. A light began to glow in the palm of his hand. With a bit of concentration he commanded, by thought alone, the action of the magical light. It floated from his palm into the cell. He cried out, ended the spell, and stumbled backwards. An acolyte, hearing the cry, came running and found the Abbot against the wall opposite the open door.

"Master?"

"The flesh—the flesh—" Stammered the Abbot.

"The sins of the flesh?" asked the acolyte, not comprehending.

The Abbot grabbed the front of the youth's robe and screamed. "No, damn you! The flesh!" He released the acolyte, pushed himself along the wall, and fled from the monks' quarters.

The acolyte was taken with more curiosity than fear or good sense and turned to the open door. He too could command the light and did so. He stepped cautiously to the door and shined the light within. In the center of the room lay Velles's discarded robe, brown, crumpled, caked with grime and sweat, hoping with lice.

Next to the robe lay Velles's discarded flesh. Where his bones, sinew, and muscle had gone, the monks would never know. The god to which the monks prayed knew, however, that Abraxas had made a successful claim.

. . .

"I can feel you grinning," said Maret. "You don't often grin."

Shall I stop?

"Please do."

You're in a foul mood today.

"How long shall we wait?"

Our time is their time.

Maret snorted. "Fine then, tell me. We have nothing else to talk about."

Tell you?

"What causes a demon to grin?"

Oh, just an old memory.

. . .

The sounds were discordant; various stringed instruments out of tune, chimes struck out of any desirable order, voices rising and falling without purpose, becoming interfering waves that struck the angel's ears and made him grimace. Tabris stood in the dappled sunlight beneath the massive elm tree, eyes closed. A slight, warm breeze passed through the edge-feathers of his pure white wings and filled his nostrils with the mingled scents of blossoming flowers. As he listened, the cacophony worked its way into a harmony. He was puzzled, puzzled over the fact that, even for a moment, anything but pure harmony could exist where he was.

He opened his eyes. The elm was on a small hill overlooking a shallow bowl of earth. To the left a steep rise of white stone, dotted with gnarled trees and wind-warped bushes, was topped with a shinning, golden temple. It reflected the sun's light to such an amplified degree it was nearly impossible to look at. To the right the depression rose to a crest of perpetually flowering trees. Just at the edge of the bowl was an assortment of believers of every intelligent race. It was they who had inexplicably slipped into disharmony.

Tabris studied them. For a fleeting moment they seemed somehow off, but he couldn't place it. The moment was gone before he had a chance to consider its implications, replaced by their playing, singing, and dancing. A shadow passed over the players. Tabris looked and saw an angel dive, bank, then beat her wings and disappear into the blinding light of the temple. He turned his attention back to the players and listened to their heavenly music.

. . .

"How is he?" hissed Abraxas.

The shadow demon, a pillar of darkness within a deep pool of shadow cast by a massive Magnolia tree, did not turn to his master. He had been ordered to watch Tabris and watch him he would. "He begins to suspect."

Abraxas slithered forward on the massive twin snakes that made-up his lower half, and peered past the shadow demon. At one end of the natural bowl Tabris watched a group of musicians and dancers.

"Must you taunt him?" asked the shadow demon.

Abraxas turned to the demon, who, in the highly fluid caste system, if there could be said to be one, was a minor player, so minor in fact that Abraxas didn't even know his name. That the demon had enough courage to question him impressed the demon lord. He looked back to Tabris.

"A guilty pleasure."

"He's observant still," said the shadow demon, "even if his mind has been shattered by his labors."

"Has he noticed *you*?" asked Abraxas.

This drew a dismissive snort from the shadow demon. The question, to his mind, wasn't worth answering. The less-than-obsequious reaction made Abraxas respect the demon still more. He made a mental note to learn what he could about the willful shadow demon then slithered over the edge of the ridge into the valley below.

. . .

The musicians paused. In the silence and stillness Tabris noticed that a second angel had come down from the tree-lined ridge. The musicians noticed as well and although they might have chosen to play a song for the newcomer they turned instead and meandered off into the valley. This act, although not necessarily rude, seemed unusual to Tabris.

"Why did they not play for you?" he asked as the second angel stepped beneath the elm.

"They follow the spirit of music, a restless spirit," said the second angel, who was, of course, Abraxas in disguise.

Tabris looked at him and recognized him at last. "Ah, Sabraxa."

"Tabris, brother," said Abraxas, stepping to Tabris and hugging him. Brother was a term of endearment and fact, as, in a sense, all angels were siblings. Despite this, no two angels could have looked more differently than these. Tabris was soft-featured, almost boyish, as if he had never matured to manhood but remained eternally innocent. His soft blonde hair flowed like snow from a mountain's peak between his shoulder blades. His pale blue eyes shown with pure intelligence even in the shadows beneath the tree. He had a preoccupied air about him, as if he were always on the verge of a profound revelation. His outward appearance masked the fact that within he was ancient beyond his years, aged by his unique, hellish experience.

Abraxas, who was again teasing Tabris, had angular features, almost those of a bird, stood upright, had the ready, alert athleticism of a warrior, and was noticeably muscular. His eyes shone a golden-green. While Tabris's wings were white, Abraxas's were various shades of yellow, green, and black and showed a pattern not unlike that of a snake. Tabris had found that unusual but thought it an inappropriate topic of conversation.

The pair enjoyed a pleasant silence, neither feeling urgency about any business, although there was urgency. Abraxas reached out and took Tabris's hand in his own. This was not an uncommon show of affection, for although many angels are aloof and aristocratic, many others are affectionate and benefit from a kind touch. Tabris was more solitary than most angels tended to be. His long years of cataloging and recording, his endless, lonesome travels, the gravity of his charge—to make a complete record of all the gods had created, seen and unseen, good and evil—had made him feel an outsider.

Upon his return he had been lauded as a hero, had been given gratuitous praise, his massive tomes taken by trembling hands and passed between the gods, who marveled over them. He had finally been "put out to pasture," as it were, to revel in his fame and glory, yet he felt alone and friendless. Abraxas knew this, and although affection was not in his nature, he knew it would benefit Tabris to receive it—it was another element of his seduction and manipulation of the fallen angel.

"Tabris, there is—," Abraxas—in angel guise—paused. Tabris turned and looked at him. "Some difficulty."

"Oh?"

"Yes," continued Abraxas. "The organizational schema poses some problems for us."

"It should be quite apparent," said Tabris.

"Yes, of course," said Abraxas. "But, brother, you must recognize that your efforts far surpassed our loftiest expectations. Your particular genius outshines all others in that regard."

Tabris patted the back of Abraxas's hand and squeezed it. "Yes, yes, forgive me. I indulged in some experimentation along the way. Also, I had to obfuscate of some of the more—dangerous material, to protect the casual reader."

"Rightfully so, brother," said Abraxas. "If you could only help us with a few passages we shall endeavor to figure out the rest on our own. I feel guilty asking that much. We all know how you've earned your respite from these books."

"Nonsense," said Tabris. "I serve my maker. My work is never done. Let us go to the great library."

. . .

Hra'Fen'Kel watched as Abraxas, a demon lord, stood hand-in-hand with an angel, a fallen angel, banished from the brilliant light of the good gods, but an angel nonetheless. The shadow demon saw both the reality and the illusion, which Tabris did not. 'Green wings, patterned after a serpent.' He shook his head. 'I warned him.' Despite the obvious tell, it was clear that Tabris remained oblivious to the truth. The pair, angel and demon, turned and headed toward the city.

. . .

He was crouched at the edge of a bubbling brook. He watched as the swift moving water ran over the varicolored rocks. Slender, brown fish raced under his gaze. Movement was reflected on the water's surface. He looked up and saw a hawk pass overhead, a long, furless tail dangling from the rat gripped in its talons. He watched as the hawk landed on a branch and peered around. Once the bird was convinced no threat was near it turned its head and looked over the still twitching body of the rat.

"I don't understand," said Maret, for she had no other name for herself. She had felt blindly along the walls of the cave, found the exit, and forced herself into the light, sound, and life of the valley.

He watched as the hawk drove its beak into the rat's side, shattering its rib cage. The hawk pulled out a mess of internal organs, threw back its head, and swallowed them.

"The natural order," he said. "One dies so another may live."

"But why?" asked Maret, not seeing the hawk, but looking at his broad, stony shoulders, thinking only of her own poorly understood situation.

"The strong beget strength into the world. The weak are sacrificed to this truth," he said, rising.

"Maret?"

He turned and faced her, looming over her. "She is strong."

"Does that make me weak?" she asked, looking up at him.

He did not answer.

"Am I going to be—"

He stepped past her, away from the hawk, toward a moon flower that held closed its blossoms. He began to examine a wheel bug that had climbed up the stalk, looking for prey. It turned its small, dark eyes to him and waved its twin antennae.

"But, I'm—" She reached out, touched his arm. He turned. She stared into his eyes. His face showed no emotion. "*Am* I Maret?" she asked. "If I'm not Maret, *who* am I? If I'm not strong I must be weak. If I'm weak—"

He reached out, extended an index finger.

"No!" she cried. She thought of turning, of bolting, like a rabbit, into the shadow and safety of vegetation, but she hesitated. She had successfully found him by ignoring the plethora of sights and sounds around her. Now that she sought safety she knew not where to turn. Everything around her bewildered her. She was overwhelmed and in being so could not act. He touched her forehead. She fainted. He caught her, lifted her, and carried her back to the cave.

. . .

The anti-paladin, Kaya, who worshiped the "angry hag," Gyronna, the goddess of extortion, hatred, and spite, sat low in her chair, her legs extended onto the plush, gold-trimmed, red carpet leading from the arched double door to the queen's throne. The grand hall was lined with those nobles who had survived Maret's quick, violent revolution. Mixed with the nobles, outnumbering them two-to-one were the once angry, previously discontented youths who had helped usher Maret into power. Kaya was the only person disrespectful enough to maintain such a posture in the queen's presence.

Maret peered down the hall from the height of her throne. Half-way to the door she saw a pair of muddy boots. As she watched, the owner knocked the heel of one boot against the toe of the other. Dry mud and not so dry horse manure fell from the boot onto the carpet. The legs drew back and Kaya's head came into view. She rotated her head from one side of the hall to the other, eyeing everyone present, her limp, green-tinted hair falling around her oval-shaped face. She flung her hair to one side, revealing her unhealthy complexion and her large eyes, one putrid yellow, the other royal purple. She looked at Maret and smiled, revealing a jumble of crooked, file-sharpened teeth. Once her presence had been noted by all in attendance she sat back and once again extended her legs.

Maret turned to Devinti, who stood beside her.

He looked at her, a knowing smile on his face. "Kaya. A paladin, ah, anti-paladin, I suppose would be the correct terminology."

"She's got brass balls," said Maret.

"She hopes you'll confront her. She would love nothing more than to trade insults with the queen," said Devinti.

"Why is she here?" asked Maret.

"She's Ramathain's lover," said Devinti. The idea sent a shiver down Maret's spine. "She is also single-handedly responsible for the massacre of the former Prince and his guards."

Maret showed surprise. "She did that—alone."

"Indeed."

Maret looked at the mud and crap-caked boots. "Invite her to diner. I would love to hear her tell of that. What's with her eyes?"

"I believe her mother is a hag."

Maret looked up at Devinti.

"Annis hag," he added.

The double doors opened. An aging, portly man with long gray hair and a clean shaven double chin stepped between the two doormen and stopped. He wore opulent red robes depicting dragons in flight. His pudgy fingers were home to two magical rings and many more non-magical. Three wands hung from his belt and his right hand gripped a sparkling blue staff, electricity arced from the staff, leaving behind the smell of burnt air. Ramathain needed no introduction.

He advanced half way down the red carpet, stopping before the outstretched legs of his half-hag lover. He turned to her, smiled, and winked. He looked to Maret, puffed out his chest and declared: "My Queen, whose rule shall last a thousand years, I have come to present to you those who survived the Red Dragon's Ordeal, the graduating class of—"

As Ramathain spoke Kaya kicked off one of her boots. She slowly, unbeknownst to Ramathain, but seen by almost everyone in the hall, begun to slip her foot under the hem of his robe. When he felt her toes against this inner thigh he choked to a stop. The hall burst out in laughter. Even Maret couldn't help but chuckle; although, she and everyone else had failed to notice that the portly wizard had not blushed.

Ramathain took a defensive step back and glared at the anti-paladin. She, in turn, pouted then bent forward and jammed her foot back into her boot.

"Do bring them in, Ramathain," said Maret once the laughter died down. Ramathain turned, went to the door, and waved his hand. A group of five students advanced into the hall. They were a mix of races and genders. They followed Ramathain to the foot of the queen's throne, all obliged to step over Kaya's legs.

A moment later, when Ramathain began to give his speech, illustrating the rigors and dangers of the Red Dragon Ordeal, a test of his own devising, the hateful half-hag began to snore. When Ramathain began to introduce his students she rose, stretched, and loudly exclaimed, "Ah, Nine Hells, this is boring." She turned to Maret. "I thought you knew how to throw a party." She looked to Ramathain, smiled, and began toward him, her two-handed sword clanking at her side. "Come on, baby, let's skip the foreplay and get right to it."

Maret looked to Devinti. The anti-paladin's behavior had to be addressed. There were moments, Maret thought, when she would rather not be queen. When she looked back to Kaya the anti-paladin had started to sprint. As she ran she drew her sword.

"Devinti!" cried Maret.

"On it!" he cried back.

The knights, standing a few steps from the throne, began to draw their own swords but Ramathain had the jump on them. The sparks arcing from his magical staff became a forked bolt of lightning. The two knights, wearing full plate, lit up, jerking spasmodically, then fell, lie motionless and began to smolder.

Maret was halfway through a spell when Kaya dove between Ramathain's students, who were themselves in the process of casting, and leapt onto the dais. She brought her sword down in a vicious overhead chop. Devinti had been quick enough and as the sword came down it slowed to a stop. A band of blue-white magical energy could be seen, bent under the unnatural strength of the half-hag. It was enough to stop the initial attack but Kaya wasn't phased. She yanked her sword back, the hilt at her hip, then thrust it forward. The tip dug into the throne. Maret wasn't there.

"Back here, bitch," growled Maret. She had *blinked* from the throne to middle of the hall. This was the effect of her first spell. She began a second. The students, momentarily confused, located her. Several spells came at her all at once. A massive ball of gelatinous fire and ash appeared directly behind her. She felt the heat against the back of her thighs. A bunch of darts, formed out of magical energy, erupted from one student's fingers, speeding unerringly toward her. A bunch of flying insects were gathering between the palms of another student's hands and would soon swarm over her, making casting almost impossible. A beam of dull gray energy shot from another student's finger but she ducked and it went high. Devinti had successfully kicked the final student—interrupting the student's casting—or she would have yet another spell to content with.

The magic missiles struck her, almost knocking her backwards into the flaming sphere. The concussive force of the bolts nearly knocked the breath from her, which should have ended her own spell, but she managed to keep the words flowing. She finished the spell just as Ramathain was spinning to face her. All around her people were beginning to scream and scramble to safety, knocking over chairs, and each other. She stepped between two overdressed women, dropped to one knee and touched the stone floor just at the edge of the carpet.

The floor shook. The stones between herself and her attackers, who, were conveniently standing close together, heaved, then shaped themselves into a rough wall, pulling the carpet with them, knocking over dozens. The wall curved at the sides and the top, forming a half shell which now contained Ramathain, Kaya, and the students. On the other side Deventi finished his own spell. A fiendish dire tiger, as tall as the throne itself and weighing as much as the dais it sat on, appeared, roared, and swiped across the group, catching one of the students and dragging her to the floor in a bloody heap. The buzzing insects she had been gathering dissipated.

Kaya turned away from the sudden stone wall to face the tiger. She glanced at Devinti.

"I'll make a cloak out of this and a rug out of you!" she hissed.

Ramathain, being close to the edge, was able to step around the wall without falling victim to the tigers's eager grasp. He grabbed a wand from his belt as he did so, lifted it, and aimed it at Maret. He said the keyword that brought the ruby tip to life. A line of fire shot from the wand. Maret *blinked*, appearing on the other side of a stunned group of onlookers. The ray of fire struck the side of a young man, burning his flesh to the bone. Ramathain frowned and began to search for Maret. Out of the corners of his eyes he saw one of his students, a dark elf male, step around the other side of the wall and point. Several wads of acid sped across the hall. Maret was forced to drop to her belly in order to dodge them, losing the spell she had begun to cast.

"Maret, get out of here!" cried Devinti. He too had begun a spell but had to give it up in order to dive behind the throne. Three of Ramathain's students had cast at him. Two of the spells struck the throne. The final, a cluster of magic missiles, curved around the throne and struck him in the shoulder. He had the immediate thought that he would buy a brooch of shielding—a magic item that absorbed such missiles—should he survive the attack.

"Ramathain, you traitor!" screamed Maret, as she struggled to her feet. She watched as the ball of fire rolled, then leapt into the air, flew over the wall. She could not see that it struck the tiger just behind the shoulder.

"If you can do it," yelled Ramathain, "why not I?" He laughed. "You were a fool to dismiss your demon, Maret. Oh? Did you think I wouldn't find out? That temper of yours will cost you." He lowered the tip of the staff and lightning arced outwards. The bolt struck first a fleeing noble, then leapt to a frightened young woman, then finally sunk into Maret's arm, instantly numbing it.

Maret heard Devinti cry out in pain. She looked but the wall of stone blocked him from view. Ramathain, in a better position, glanced over his shoulder, then looked back to Maret.

"Seems my lover has killed yours."

Maret began a spell. Even the crackle and pain of another of Ramathain's bolts did not stop her. When she finished the powerful necromantic spell an unearthly hush fell over the room. Ramathain staggered back. The dark elf fell to his knees, clutching at his chest. Ramathain turned and dove behind the stone wall. Not that it mattered. The spell knew where he was, it could feel the water in his corpulent body, and it wanted it. Maret watched as the dark elf, the only one affected by the spell she could see, began to wilt like a plant enduring a season-long drought in an instant. His flesh clung to his body, taunt, leathery. Then it began to grow brittle and crack. Finally, as the dark elf fell forward, his entire body began to flake away. When he struck the floor he burst into a cloud of dust. All that was left behind were his bones and pure white hair.

Her anger spent, Maret finally felt the effect of the magical lightning. Pain flowed through her body like bad blood, turning her stomach. She doubled over and vomited. Her head spun and all she wanted to do was lie down in her bed. She forced herself toward the wall, half falling on it for support. She peered around the edge. Her spell, appropriately called *horrid wilting*, had turned the remainder of Ramathain's students to dust. Only the student killed by the dire tiger escaped that horrible fate and she had accomplished that by dying first.

Ramathain himself had not entirely turned to dust. He was, however, mortally wounded. He lie on his side, his robes deflated, as he had been drastically desiccated. He appeared to be reaching out to Kaya, who sat on the edge of the dais, her back turned, holding onto something. The dire tiger lay beside her, panting its final breaths.

Maret staggered to the edge of the dais and sat down. She ran through the spells she had memorized that morning, searching for one that was relatively easy to cast yet that would finish Kaya.

"He's quite handsome," said Kaya.

Maret turned and saw that Kaya held Devinti's broken body, his head in her lap.

"Damn you," growled Maret, rising and staggering to the other woman. She grabbed the half-hag's shoulder and spun her, or attempted to. When she pulled on the woman's shoulder something hot, red, and liquid gushed from the woman's side. Maret recognized intestines when she saw them. Kaya looked up at her, smiled weakly, then looked down at her own guts. She looked at Devinti, then the tiger.

"Managed to get both," she said, extending one arm and burying her blood-soaked hand into the tiger's short mane. She ran the fingers of her other hand through Devinti's black hair. "Didn't expect to fight such a fierce beast. Never can predict anything when it comes to wizards. Say," she looked up at Maret, "you don't know any healing spells, do you? All I have are inflict." She turned to look at the tiger and fell sideways, her head falling on his. The tiger, his great black eyes staring vacantly, panted several more times, then stopped. His body began to dematerialize. When he was gone, an after effect of the summons spell, the anti-paladin fell further, her head knocking on the stone.

Maret could now see Devinti. He lay on his back, his head in the dead anti-paladin's lap. His chest had been cut open by her blade, his heart sliced in two. She stepped onto the dais and took him from the half-hag's lap to her own and began to cry.

Half an hour later she was still crying. The hall was empty of all life except her. Ramathain had died, although she hadn't yet noticed. A knight appeared at the door. "Queen? Queen Maret?"

Maret looked up but saw only the stone half-shell. "Here," she said, then looked back down at Devinti. The knight ran around the wall. His sword was drawn and covered in blood, as was his armor. He took off his helmet. "Queen, the people have risen against you. They storm the castle. We've turned them away but—" He finally seemed to comprehend the scene before him. "Queen?"

. . .

The monastery appeared to have fallen into ruin. The town nearby, after suffering plague after plague of snakes, had been abandoned. Even the road that passed nearby had largely been forgotten and was now overgrown. Within the monastery the monks and clerics, who once followed the disciplined path to self-perfection prescribed by Irori, now debased themselves in service to Abraxas.

The change had come slowly. A monk had disappeared, or had mysteriously been killed, none knew, and left behind a blasphemous tome. The book had been put to the flames and the ashes scattered. The followers of Irori tried to put the episode behind them but found they could not. The blasphemous content from the destroyed book turned up in other books, nestled within the sacred texts, blending with the sacred words.

Slowly, over years, the words penned by Velles, dictated to him by Abraxas, edged out the teachings of Irori. A decade later and the library of the monastery held nothing but the teachings of Abraxas; the dark, corrupting thoughts he passed on to all of his followers. Finally, Abraxas's will was revealed to the monks and clerics. He wanted them to do something for him, something incredibly dangerous but well suited to their particular strengths. He wanted them to collect the scattered pages of the *Book of the Damned*.

That sacred calling would occupy the monastery for the next two decades. It would result in the death of three-fourths their number. Still, with unheard of self sacrifice on the part of the monks and clerics, and all the aid Abraxas could safely give them, the book had come together. Abraxas knew, from experience, that the book never stayed together long. Some working of the book itself kept it scattered, as if that were the only way to keep itself safe. He knew this because this was the third time he had managed to successfully gather all of the pages. He had often, in the thousands of years since the books dispersal, had possession, via his followers, of individual pages. He had never seen one himself. That, he knew, was too dangerous. No, he had done before as he had done now, used proxies.

In the past he had employed a succubus to seduce a powerful warlord. This warlord, Uz, and his half-fiend children, had gathered the book. This was before Nex sieged Absalom, some four millennia prior. Centuries later, when Tar-Baphon was mortally wounded by Aroden, cultists of Abraxas snuck into Tar-Baphon's personal study and stole the *Book of the Damned* from him. A great passage of time lay between then and now. Many individual pages had passed through the hands of his servants. Much had been learned and added to his own library. Abraxas was patient. Under his direction the monks and clerics would learn what they could from the book and he would add more to his copy.

. . .

"She must hide," said Velles.

Zucra, also known as the Twisted Mouth—although never to her face—was a marilith: serpent from the waist down, from the waist up a six armed humanoid female. A demon of marked ferocity. She stared at the glabrezu with her pupil-less eyes. Velles—now a glabrezu, a bipedal demon with four arms, two of them massive, ending in claws, and two the size and shape of human arms—was physically larger than the marilith, yet he was crouching down, making himself as small as he could. He may be larger, but a Zucra, really, any marilith, but especially this one, was far more powerful.

"She is under threat."

"If she cannot defend herself," said the marilith, "she is too weak to be of concern."

"It's not that. She needs something only Abraxas can provide."

"Abraxas is not to be disturbed."

"I know," said Velles, "he has the *Book of the Damned*."

Zucra arched an eyebrow. Her three pairs of arms folded across her chest. "How do you know that?"

Velles grinned. "I helped him acquire it. When the book was finally assembled he illuminated my dark heart with the joy of success. He also promised advancement. A balor, perhaps."

Zucra rocked back on her serpentine lower half. "You—a balor?" Her twisted lips attempted a frown. All that was available to her was a grimace. "Tell me what it is you want. Perhaps Abraxas shall hear it, perhaps not."

"Maret has made a shabti, or rather, has caused a shabti to be made. It is close to ready and will soon go before Pharasma."

"A foolish plan," interrupted Zucra. "Pharasma will detect the ruse. Why bother?"

"Phrasma will only see the truth if she can feel that what is before her is not wholly and completely Maret. If she cannot sense the true Maret, how will she know that the shabti is a fake?"

"Oh?" replied Zucra. "And how will you hide Maret's true soul from the Lady of Graves? Where in the multiverse can the goddess of life and death not see?"

Velles grinned again. It was becoming a habit. "Into the *Book of the Damned*."

. . .

Three women stood beneath the enviably named "tree of heaven," rubbing the sleep from their eyes, waiting for the queen to appear. The tree's smooth, brown bark and pinnate leaves were nearly lost, along with the women, in the pre-dawn darkness. Only the moon's dim glow as it hugged the horizon illuminated the garden. When Maret was informed by the royal gardener, kept over from the now dead king's administration, of the tree's genus she chose it as the spot for her early morning obediences to Abraxas.

The women roused when a tall, dark-haired, dark-complexioned, dark-eyed, Garundian cleric of Norgorber

—the mysterious god of greed, murder, secrets, and poison —came into view. A hasty alliance had been struck so as to keep the dangerous church from joining the opposing side of the growing rebellion. This particular cleric, the highest ranking priest in the region, had become Maret's adviser, replacing Devinti. Maret was taking no chances since the attack by Ramathain, his lover, students, and the larger attack on the castle by the populous. The cleric was followed by an armed guard. Maret followed this pair, flanked by two more armed guards.

The cleric, who went by the name Meidau, which, in Infernal, meant "death by exsanguination," stood next to the trio of singers. The guards took up strategic positions around the small clearing. Maret, carrying a dagger in her right hand, crossed the clearing and stepped between the three women, who moved to make room for her. Maret studied the branches of the tree of heaven, found one that suited her purpose, and cut it free. She then handed the dagger to Meidau, who put it back in the empty sheath at his belt.

No one spoke.

Maret wore an open-front robe. She was nude beneath. She swept the robe behind her and knelt on the gravel. Her face was taunt with resolve and the expectation of pain. She held the branch above her, head bent, eyes on her own heavily scarred thighs. Meidau looked at the three women and nodded.

The women began the otherworldly chorus, a song mimicking the ambient sounds of the Abyss. Maret closed her eyes. At the first high-pitched wail Maret brought down the branch against her thighs. When the branch struck she said a single, forbidden, mystical word, one of many she would utter during her obedience. Hearing the word stung the singers' ears. They raised their voices to drown out the remainder.

Maret was usually patient, sadistic, even methodical in her self-flagellation. This morning she was emotional. The flesh on her thighs became a patchwork of bruises, welts, and cuts. When her scars began to open, the blood flowed at an alarming rate. Maret no longer chanted the words, she screamed them. The blood-painted leaves of the branch flew free, clinging to her legs, arms, and abdomen. Blood soaked the gravel and formed a pool beneath her. No one interfered.

Her vision blurred. The thrashing of the branch faded away, although she still felt the sting. The song of the three singers became an increasingly distant sound, until it disappeared completely. Maret no longer saw the trees, bushes, and flowers of the garden. She no longer felt the rocks beneath her knees. The sun was breaking over the crest of a hill. She looked up and saw the silhouette of an abandoned monastery, walls crumbling, overgrown with vines.

A deep, throbbing bass came from the top of the hill. She rose and began to climb. She passed through a gap in the wall, entering a weed-choked courtyard. Within the walls of the monastery the thumping bass was overwhelming. It rattled her teeth and made her joints hurt. She was able to pinpoint the direction it came from and turned that way, arriving at a pair of open doors. There was only darkness within. Not even the sun's light passed the threshold. It was as if a black felt curtain hung just behind the doors.

She reached out and attempted to run her fingers along the unnatural barrier of darkness. It offered no resistance. She stepped in. At first she saw nothing. The volume of the beating increased. She felt it in her bones. Something brushed against her. She recoiled. Another form brushed past her, this time she caught the faint, bluish hue. It was followed by another, then another. Maret could make out humanoid forms, souls, flying through the darkness. She was reminded of those she had sacrificed, captured, and had seen after their release. The souls came from behind her, passed by her, cold and lifeless. She followed them.

The souls were traveling down a hall the dimensions of which Maret could not discern. The hall led to a large room. Upon entering the room, the souls slithered on the floor like snakes, pouring over the lip of a bottomless pit. Within the room the rhythmic beating was almost deafening. Maret noticed one end of a chain was anchored to the stone floor. She followed its length with her eyes. The chain shot off into the darkness, joined by dozens of others she began to pick out of the gloom.

Maret stepped forward, to the edge of the pit. Below, hundreds of souls swam, a terrifying shoal. As Maret watched, several souls broke formation and emerged from the pit. They floated into the air, their blue light illuminating the source of the repetitive bass; a massive heart, covered in glowing runes, straining against its chains.

"The heart—," said one of the souls, as it floated down and stopped next to her. She turned and looked but the soul leapt into the air and flew down the hall, disappearing from view.

"Of the ancient evil—," said another soul, stepping next to Maret. She spun. It glanced at her, then bent like a runner, launched, and sped down the hall.

"Powers the—," said yet another soul, pirouetting around her, turning, and speeding off. Maret watched it follow its companions. She awaited the rest of the statement and although other souls flew around the heart, none stepped to the edge of the pit. Instead, they appealed to her, reaching out.

"Come," said one.

"To us," said another.

"We will know you."

"Come to us, Maret."

"Join us."

"Join us, Maret."

"Read the words upon the heart and rejoice, for your end is near."

The bass of the beating heart was slowly replaced with the treble of the branch cutting through the air and striking her flesh. The howling of the souls was superseded with her own agonizing cries. The heart, the bottomless pit, and the seducing souls faded from view. She awoke in her royal chambers, Meidau standing over her, a look of admiration on his face.

"I've witnessed captives beaten into unconsciousness," he said. "Now I've had the pleasure of witnessing one to it to oneself. Magnificent."

"Send my body servant," said Maret. "To draw my bath."

"The revolution?" asked Meidau.

"After my bath."

"As you wish."

. . .

Maret, the shabti, but no longer aware of her own fictitious nature, now wholly believing her forced identity, and wholly ignorant of the truth of her existence, attempted to read the emotions displayed on the stone face. It stared from the concave bowl in the cave wall, his aloof, aristocratic features perfectly sculpted and perfectly enigmatic. He stared through her for what felt like an eternity. Only when her patience was coming to an end did a smirk curl his lips.

"It cannot be done," he said. "Your soul is not your own. Nor is its ultimate fate mine to meddle with."

"Maybe you're afraid," said Maret. "I've spent my life rooting out the weakness in my own heart only to find it all around me. I don't need you. I'll tell Pharasma to go to Hell."

"Perhaps she shall say the same to you."

Maret wished she could turn her back to him. Instead, she began to shimmy from the narrow cave. Just as she began to see the angled light pouring into the cave entrance his face, neck, and shoulders emerged, cutting off her exit. He turned his head to face her, his lips just at her ear. She could not even turn her head for fear of touching her lips to his. Nor did she retreat into the cave, unwilling to show weakness.

"Do you remember your creation?" he asked.

"I don't have time for games."

"Do you recall that I wept for you?" he asked.

"I can't imagine why."

"Would you deny your creator?" he asked.

"I don't know. Who created me?" asked Maret.

"I did."

"Get out of my way," said Maret.

He sank back into the stone, his eyes on her until the last.

"Unbelievable," she said, and shimmied from the cave.

As she arrived at the mouth she called out to her demon companion. "You've wasted our time. He won't do it, or can't." She paused, listening. *He* felt strangely absent, as absent as the songs of the birds and the chatter of the insects. She listened. What had once been a vibrant chorus of life was now mute. She peered out and looked upon a barren landscape. She stepped out of the cave. There was only stone and the howl of wind as it swept through the vacant valley, rustling her hair and robes. She began a spell but before she could cast it a pair of hands grabbed her ankles.

She looked down. The hands were stone, had come up from the stone, and they were far from alone. The entire valley floor sprouted similar stone hands. She tried to yank her feet free but found herself held fast. The hands nearby reached, emerging on stone arms, to grab her legs, to yank her down. She fell among the hands and screamed as they grabbed her arms, legs, torso. They squeezed and tore. She felt a chunk of flesh rip free from her calf. The hand that had wounded her sunk into the rock, taking its prize with it. A hand grabbed her hair and pulled her head to the rock. Another grabbed the back of her neck. She became panicked, forgot her spells, and screamed for help.

The hands continued their work. She felt her bones snap in their pitiless grip, felt herself being pulled to pieces. The stone hands were ruthlessly efficient. Before long her screams became whimpers, then silence. The hands, clutching the wet, sticky, soft parts of Maret, retreated into the stone, leaving only a smear of blood. Her blood soaked into the stone like moisture into desert pavement. Only minutes after Maret had left the cave she and all signs of her life and death were gone.

From the cave there came the sound of weeping. The shabti's creator stood in shadow, looking out. He had created the shabti, filled it with Maret's sin, and now he had destroyed it. Tears ran down his cheeks. It had, he thought, been a disagreeable task.

. . .

Maret, the shabti, although she believed herself to be Maret proper, opened her eyes and saw an unbelievable scene. She was crowded together with a countless multitude. Before her two men dressed in ornate robes of gold, on which images of the lives of the saints—or of the martyrdom of the individual himself—had been embroidered, held the limp body of a third man. They lowered it down. The man, who, judging by the pallor of his flesh, was dead, wore elaborate, gilded armor and a cloak of ermine. Around the man stood a crowd of grief-stricken nobility. A priest wearing a diaphanous gown over his black robes began to recite verse from *The Bones Land in a Spiral*.

Rising above the funeral scene was a host of angels, saints, and souls. They floated on the ether. Behind them, the star-dotted sky rose in a fantastic dome. In the distance a massive white spire glowed with its own inner light. Above this assorted group sat a plump, middle-aged woman, her brown hair shot through with silver. She wore a simple dress and had no raiment yet it was obvious she was both wise and powerful, as all deferred to her. The funeral scene faded, leaving only the soul, which knelt before Pharasma and her host.

Several of those crowded around Maret whispered to each other, she overhearing.

"A king."

"Who?"

"No, a count."

"Not a king?"

"Pretensions to be king, perhaps."

"Count Orgaz."

"Why does he get to—"

"Just because he's nobility?"

"Fool, he's been waiting here for who knows how long. You simply didn't see him."

"Why the funeral scene?"

"A bit of theatrics, to bolster his case."

There seemed to be some passionate talk amongst the saints. One, a man who wore the rough-made cloth of a desert hermit, was arguing on behalf of the count. Another, an angel with wings of gold-hued feathers, argued against.

A soul, that of a woman who bore a resemblance to the count, sat nearby watching the proceeding. Those other souls in attendance, as well as the saints and the angels, all spoke, taking sides, as it were. Some, emboldened perhaps by long residencies, called out their opinions to Pharasma. Final judgment, it seemed, was a noisy, chaotic affair.

Despite the disorder, Pharasma was unperturbed. She did not silence those in attendance, but sat listening as the sins and virtuous acts of Count Orgaz were presented. After a lengthy appeal by the hermit she raised a hand. The multitude grew quiet. Pharasma sat forward and spoke to the soul that had once been a count.

"The saints are for you. The angels against." A knowing smile crossed her lips. "I have found that man is sympathetic to man, while those who have never struggled with the temptation to sin are quick to condemn." She sat back. "I am told that when you died a miracle occurred, that two of my chosen," here she turned and scanned the crowd to her left, spotting the two of whom she spoke, "descended to lower your body into the grave. This was shown to me just now. Your good works commend you. Let the Heavenly archons guide you to your final abode." She nodded and Count Orgaz's soul faded from view.

The scantily clad hermit turned and waved to Maret.

"What!" Cried out one of those waiting to be judged.

"She's just gotten—"

"Unconscionable!"

"A scandal! She's waited but a moment."

"Why be in a hurry? Are you so certain of a good outcome?"

The multitude fell to silence as Maret stepped from the crowd and stood alone before the assembled souls, angels, and saints. The hermit looked down at her, a frown on his wizened face. The gold-feathered angel did not look, but turned his face away. The saints studied her, then began to whisper amongst themselves. The hermit turned his face to Pharsma, who looked at him. What silent understanding passed between them Maret could not fathom. Pharasma looked at Maret, her brow furrowed.

. . .

A young woman, a recent addition to the queen's household staff, hand-picked by Meidau, knocked gently on the door of the bedchamber. Hearing no response she opened the door and peered in. She saw no one and entered. She went to the bed and saw the queen's sleep-stilled figure beneath the blankets.

"My Queen?" she asked, reaching out and placing her hand on Maret's scar-covered thigh. "I have drawn a bath. My Queen?" She shook Maret, who woke with a start. Her body's reaction to her self-inflicted pain had sent her into a light doze. She regarded the young woman. "Your bath, my Queen."

Maret rose from her bed, the blood-soaked sheets clinging to her legs. She reached and yanked them free. She took the arm of the young woman and was helped to her tub. The young woman, her body servant, aided her into the bath.

"Forgive me for asking, my Queen, but what has happened to you?" The young woman watched as the blood from Maret's wounds swirled into the bath water, rivulets of red rising to the surface.

Maret looked at her body servant. "One must pay a price for knowledge and power."

The girl went to a small table and retrieved a sponge. She returned and knelt by the tub's side. "I wouldn't know anything about that, my Queen," she said, as she wetted the sponge and began to gently wash Maret with it. "I'm a simple woman." She glanced at Maret but looked back to the sponge. "The daughter of a former—" She fell silent.

Maret rest her head on the edge of the tub and closed her eyes. Her body servant continued to wash her. After a few minutes she rose and went again to the small table. She lifted the edge of a towel which exposed the handle of a black-bladed dagger. She looked over her shoulder at Maret, who still lay with her head back, her eyes closed.

The young woman lifted the towel with her left hand and let it unfold. She lifted the dagger with her right hand and hid it behind the towel. She walked to the edge of the tub and stood looking down into the pink water.

"My father was a minor noble," she said, now looking at Maret, who did not open her eyes. "When you took power my father and brothers were slaughtered by those young men who—"

Maret opened her eyes and tilted her head to look at her body servant. The young woman did not keep Maret's gaze but looked absently into the bloody, soapy water.

"I was taken and sold to the temple of Norgorber, a slave." Now she looked at Maret. "I don't know what happened to my mother or sister."

Maret, not liking the topic, began to rise.

"Here," said her body servant, "let me dry you." She reached out with the towel. Maret watched her. The expression on the young woman's face never changed from grief and sadness, not even when she dropped the towel, it landing half in the water, half out, and plunged the enchanted, poisoned dagger into Maret's chest. She reached out, releasing the dagger's handle, and grabbed Maret. She helped Maret slide back into the tub, she herself kneeling at its side.

"Meidau promised I could get revenge," said the young woman, looking into Maret's eyes. "For all you've done to my family. He promised freedom." She stood and pulled the dagger free. A gurgling spout of blood exited the wound, splashing into the cooling water of the bath. "But I don't want to live anymore." The young woman plunged the dagger into her own heart. She staggered backwards, wavered, then crumpled.

Maret, covering her wound with both hands, whispered *his* name. "How could you—" She coughed up blood. "Have let—" She felt intense heat radiating from the wound in her chest followed by waves of cold. She slid down in the tub until she rest at the bottom, looking up from below with lifeless eyes.

. . .

Abraxas is pleased. He sent you a vision of your fate. Did you hear the beating of the dark heart? He will hide you in the—

Velles stood at the head of the tub. He looked into the water. It was so mixed with blood he could barely see Maret at the bottom. He looked to the side and saw the crumpled body of the young woman.

. . .

The Abyss had been waiting to claim Maret's soul. She had, through various forbidden rites, pledged her soul to that poisoned land. In return for ownership of her soul, Maret had received an advance. She was granted an extended youth, knowledge of things no mortal should know, and power far beyond anything she could have acquired on her own—or even imagined. Yet, when the Abyss reached out, it found that another had taken Maret's soul. It raged.

. . .

"A balor, eh?" Zucra asked, looking at Velles. "A lemure, perhaps."

"Something's gone terribly wrong. I need to speak with Abraxas immediately."

"He doesn't have time for those who've failed him."

. . .

"You have no power over me!" screamed Maret, the shabti, believing her words to be the truth. "I'm bound to Abraxas, to the Abyss itself. Why am I here? I'm soon to be a demon, torturing pathetic souls like these!" Maret waved behind her, indicated the crowd of waiting souls, who cried out in disgruntled protest.

Pharasma, the hermit, and the assembled saints listened to her diatribe with strained patience. The angels looked on with pity. Just then a twin appeared. Maret looked upon herself. The assembled saints gasped in surprise. A great furor arose in those present. Even the angels appeared at a loss to comprehend the appearance of a "second" soul. Pharasma leaned forward, looked back and forth between Maret and her shabti, then reclined.

"We may begin."

. . .

An angel, who had for eons taken a body of earth, sat with his back to the valley wall. The sky above was paused in twilight, the sky above mirroring the mood within. The valley, once as verdant as the First World, was now lifeless stone. All was silent until a strange sound began to echo down the valley's length. It was as if a hundred hunting horns called forth. It heralded a prosecution. The stone-angel frowned. The valley filled with brilliant light; which, settled down to something like the breaking of dawn. The stone-bodied-angel shook his head, frowned, and looked away from the source of the light.

"You have been warned." Came a voice from the light, a voice that sounded similar to his own. "You have been banished. Now you must return to face judgment."

"Wasn't banishment judgment?" asked the stone-bodied-angel, turning and looking up. A muscular angel in shining armor, his gold-feathered wings folded behind him, loomed over the stone-bodied-angel, his brethren, sword in-hand.

"It was mercy and an opportunity," said the prosecutor, who had been sent by Pharasma to fetch the wayward sibling. "You should have been redeeming yourself, not proving yourself a vain fool."

"Are *you* your brother's keeper?" asked the stone-bodied-angel. The prosecutor was about to speak, but the stone-bodied-angel waved a hand and began to rise. "It doesn't matter."

"You acquiesce?"

"Put away your naked blade."

The stone-bodied-angel, now standing, began to follow the prosecutor toward the pillar of light. Just as they reached the magical gate to the Boneyard the stone-bodied-angel stopped, turned, and looked out over the valley. The prosecutor gripped his still-drawn sword. The stone-bodied-angel moved his hand in a wide arc. The valley sprang to life. He knelt and held out his hand. A copper-colored fox jogged forward and sniffed his fingers. He hazarded a single friendly lick. The stone flesh of the banished angel began to crack and flake away. The fox turned, stepped quickly, turned again and watched as the angel's true form was revealed. The fox gazed upon twins.

. . .

Just as before, there was only void. Then came sensation. Then the power of the word.

"You are never responsible for the actions of others."

Pharasma's voice filled the valley. Maret, for she had no other name for herself, lay not on stone but on something pleasantly soft.

"You are only responsible for yourself."

The welcoming sounds of nature filled Maret's ears. The sweet fragrances of flowers filled her nostrils. Beneath her hands was life-bearing soil, blanketed with clover.

"Go forth to live and act, yet remember that soon you shall be judged."

Maret opened her eyes. The familiar valley walls rose to either side. She had perfect recall of all that her short life had been. She was created not by nature or by the will of the divine, but by a sub-archon, who thought himself greater than he was. She had been filled with the sins of another and made to stand judgment in her place. Those sins had been returned to their rightful owner. While the sins of Maret had left, the portion of her soul that animated her shabti remained. Like a gas it expanded to fill its container. That container was now free to, as Pharasma had commanded, live and act.

The ploy had failed.

One cannot trick a god.

H. Rad Bethlen has been compared to Isak Dinesen (*Seven Gothic Tales*) and Fritz Leiber (*Ill Met in Lankhmar*). He is known for his work in the fantasy and horror genres as well as his non-fiction. He has been published in Europe and America.

For more great fiction and non-fiction please visit:

roosterandravenpublishing.com

hradbethlen.com

or H. Rad Bethlen's Amazon page.

www.ingramcontent.com/pod-product-compliance
Lightning Source LLC
LaVergne TN
LVHW011051110826
845149LV00015B/3460

* 9 7 8 1 9 6 5 6 5 0 4 5 5 *